THE QUANTUM TRIO

FIGHT FOR THE SUPERMINDS

ATHARV GARG

Contents

INTRODUCTION

It is my pleasure to introduce myself as Dr. Cyrus Celdon. Dr. CC is the name I am usually known by. The creative agency Cosmos X employs me as a member of their team. As a result of our research, we can learn more about outer space and the planets of our universe.

CHAPTER ONE

CYRUS CELDON

Dr. CC was an ordinary man with a small shop of grocery. On 5 September 1999, his brother 'Albus Celdon' died from a mystery. The next day Mr. CC had a dream in which his brother told him about Cosmos X and told him to check his IQ and apply for CosmosX. He didn't believe it at first. After every two days, he had the same nightmare.

He was fed up with it and finally did the same. He searched about Cosmos X and got interested in it. He checked his IQ and was shocked to know that his IQ was 155.

IQ = mental age x chronological age x 100.

He applied for Cosmos X and cleared two rounds with ease. He was selected for training and study about outer space. Furthermore, he is 65 yearold; he has a big white curly beard, is 6.2 ft in height, always wears a brown coat, has blue eyes, and is bald.

He has been working for Cosmos X since 2002. He has a secret that he can predict the future. This power came to him when he studied astronomy and lived a monk's lifestyle. He is a passionate man and can do whatever he wants to.

He is an unsolvable man. You cannot guess his next move.

CHAPTER TWO

New Discovery

It's the date 11 December 2015; Dr. CC is now the chairman of Cosmos X. He has launched a telescope satellite called BigCurrent. It can capture images 100x zoomed. On 10 April 2016, BigCurrent captured a picture of a planet similar to Earth which has one thin ring around it.

The Planet was named Kepler-452b by the outer space community. With this image, Dr. CC hadsuspicious thinking and made this planet his mission. Years passed, but nothing new about this planet was discovered.

This mission took about 5 million dollars. Everyone thought through this planet, we would attain nothing. The Outer space community put pressure on Cosmos X and mainly on Dr. CC.

This project was now closed because of the force. 9 December 2019 was the date when it was the last date for this mission. DR. CC was quite sad because this mission meant a lot to him.

CHAPTER THREE

ALBUS CELDON

He had a nightmare that night in which his brother was in danger. He is being chased by many people who look like they live on another planet. Albus says only, -Help me!!!'.

*Dr. CC had the same dream every day. It is now the 3rd day Dr. CC had the same nightmare, but his brother said, -Help Me!! I am on.' *Beep beep* (a sound from Albus's background)*

Dr. CC went to his monk trainer and asked for help. He wanted to talk to someone dead. His trainer asked Dr. CC whom you have to speak to. Dr. CC replied, 'to my brother.'. The monk said, "Who said that he is dead" with some fishy accent. Dr. CC said, "please, Sir, I have to talk to my brother. Please guide me in some way." Monk said, "Ok, I can give you this power for only five minutes.

Otherwise, your body will get a lot of pressure, and your body might blast.". Dr. CC goes into a meditation position and thinks about his brother. Soon after, he feels that his brother is sitting in front of him, but it's his brother's soul. Dr. CC asked, "Are you alive? Where are you? Are you fine?" and many such questions.

Albus answered, "We don't have much time. I want to say that I am alive and okay. I want a favour from you that you may go to the house and find a luminous gemstone that shines when light falls on it. Create a device in which the light always falls on it." Albus continued, "Because of it, we can communicate." At the next moment, the monk wakes r. CC. Dr. CC leaves without saying anything to his home.

CHAPTER FOUR

THE COMMUNICATION INVENTION

Dr. CC reached the home and opened things of Albus. In that, a blue-yellow gradient bag was found. He opened the bag and found the luminous gemstone; a slip was attached. It was written in the Japanese language. It was "通信血液." Dr. CC translated, and it came to know, "communicate blood.". In the front zip, a letter was found. The letter said, "Whoever founds

The-Communicate-Blood, is not a standard gemstone. By creating this device, it has the power to communicate with each other but of blood relation.". The following page was written about how to build the machine. To transmit, you have to make a device in which aaser light would reflect millions of times. The light should be white and should never stop.

Dr. CC made a device that looked like a dice. Mirrors covered the front of the dice, which contained a miniature of the sun. The 'communicate blood' was held in the centre. A ray came from the dice, and Dr. CC could see Albus. After two minutes, the beam was gone. Then Dr. CC read the last page of the letter. On it, the rules were written. The main limitation was it could function only for two minutes. On the very next day, Dr. CC talked to Albus. Albus told him, "We both are the main warriors to save our civilization from its end."

THE URGENCY OF WARRIORS

Every day Albus says the same thing. But today, he said, "I am telling you the secret. I am on the planet which is similar to Earth and has, they have come!!!!" and yelled. The call gets over, and Dr. CC is afraid for his brother.

He has troubling questions, such as: "Who are they? Why he hung up the call?" and many others. For 3 - 4 days, they didn't talk to each other, but on the fourth night, the beam came from the dice. Dr. CC ran and talked to Albus.

Albus said, "We don't have much time. I want to say that I am on a planet similar to Earth and has thin rings around it Its real name is arth2010. Please create an army of three 14 - 15-year-old children with superpowers." When Dr. CC wanted to say something, the call was declined. Dr. CC was sure that planet is Kepler-452b Dr. CC had many doubts but was not thinking of them; he just started finding super intelligent kids, as Dr. CC knew they would not have superpowers.

CHAPTER SIX

THE 1ST IMPERIUM CHILD

Dr. CC held a contest in the United States of America. The Olympiad was related to science and math. In the Olympiad, you only have 30 minutes, and you have to solve 60 challenging questions.

Dr. CC was held at the entry gate of the centre and saw a girl of about 15 years of age. She was confident, had red eyes, and her height was about 5.8 ft. She wore a white t-shirt, a black skirt, and a black varsity jacket. She also had a gemstone in her head. Dr. CC thought that she was the one who would join us.

After the Olympiad, Dr. CC announced the highest marks, which were 280 out of 300 and were of the same girl. Her name is Ivory. Dr. CC offers to join her. She said, "I will have to ask my elder sister, who is like a mother to me." She asks for some time to ask her sister.

Likewise, she went to her sister and took her to Dr. CC. Her sister agreed to Dr. CC. Her sister also asked for a promise that He would keep Ivory safe and told Dr. CC that her life *is only based on the gemstone; it is named 'Hearty' by me.*

They both headed off to a friend of Dr. CC's. His friend can read anyone's mind but can't control it. His friend's name is "Eden." When Eden meets Ivory, he is shocked that Ivory has the power to see traps through her gemstone and control the minds of anyone. Eden asks, "do you ever feel pain in the gemstone and get dizzy when you see brick form."

Ivory replies, "Yes, but why are you asking." Eden said, "You can see traps in the path and control the mind. You will only help in saving our civilization from some great danger." Ivory said, "I am only an ordinary girl. I can't do all this which you told us." Eden told Dr. CC that we only have to help her realize her power by fear of her.

Eden knew that his master told him about Ivory only. Eden's master said to him that he would train a girl with a gemstone in her head. Eden told Ivory to meditate They will throw bricks toward her if she dodges them then she realizes the power of the Hearty. Then Eden told Ivory to see in his eyes and tell him something to do in her brain.

Ivory did the same. When they throw bricks toward her, she dodges them with ease. The Hearty shines in orange colour. Ivory feels motivated and says she can see a trap in the door of his house. Eden jumps with excitement. Then Ivory does as he speaks. Ivory told Eden to bring her a glass of water. For the first time, it didn't work. But the third time, Ivory eyes shone in red colour, and Eden brought a glass of water for Ivory. Ivory realized her superpowers. Ivory is now super confident.

Eden said that she was the symbol of fire and mind.

CHAPTER SEVEN

MAGIC WITH CX

Dr. CC talks to Albus and learns there will be a war between aliens and humans. Albus said, "The Heroshamin are going to attack the Earth with his great army. It is the alien living on Kepler-452b. Please create a team of three children with superpowers.".

Then Dr. CC asks Albus, "Why only three children?". Albus replies, "I will tell you when you will create the team. Bye!!". Dr. CC now wants to create a team and learn about Heroshamin. He looked around in his laboratory in the head department of Cosmos X. Dr. CC thought he must visit other countries. He first went to Germany. Then he went to Britain.

There he saw that HARRY POTTER was quite famous. Then he saw a girl with a wand and an 'X' on hehand. Dr. CC talked to her and asked if her mark was real or if she had made it. From the back, her mother said, "It is real." Dr. CC asked, "But why? Please tell me more about her." Her mother asked, "Why do you want to know about my sugarplum."

Dr. CC replied, "I am making a team of children with superpowers. When I saw your daughter, I had an aura like someone with any superpower was there." Her mother said, "Ok, I willtell you; my daughter's name is Zara. She was born with an "X" mark on her hand." Zara's mother continued, when she was ten days old, she was sleeping at night, and in the morning, she got a wand in her hand.

Nobody knew the wand came from. Zara loves to play with the wand. Zara also kept the wand's name CX. Zara sometimes does magic whenever someone hits on her mark. The magic is harmful. Zara now has control of her agic, but she never uses it to harm someone. Zara feels insecure without CX."

Dr. CC said, -Wow, that's amazing we were finding a person like Zara only. " Dr. CC asked, "My lady If you allow me to take your daughter for a great mission for the sake of human civilization?" Zara's mother replied, "I can't believe you. I met you just 15 minutes ago; I need to know you. Please tell me about yourself. "

Dr. CC said, "My name is Cyrus Celdon. I am 66 years old. I am the chairman of Cosmos X. I live in California, USA. Furthermore, I am a trustworthy person. Not only that, but I don't have any criminal record. Wikipedia has also stated me on their website. The Times of India have written an article on me too."

Zara's mother replied, "I believe you. I am ready to give my daughter to you. I have asked Zara, and she is ready. Now you are only the teacher of my sugarplum." Zara said, "I am ready to go with you and want to help you in your mission." Then Zara and Dr. CC went back to Laboratory. Then Zara met Ivory. They both became friends quite early and started practicing with each other. During the practice, Zara learned a new skill of healing anyone.

CHAPTER EIGHT

THE QUANTUM TRIO

Then the next week, Dr.CC, with Ivory and Zara, headed off to India. Dr. CC had heard the news that a child of age 14 years had gained powers from lord Shree Hanuman by chanting the name Shree Ram. His name has been noted in The World Daily. His name is Samarth. His punch can break ten bricks and one tree at one time. He can do a long jump of 1000 cm, whereas A normal can only jump about 250 cm. Samarth jumps four times higher than most people. Shree Hanuman's tail is all Samarth wants. Currently, he resides in Bengaluru, India.

As Dr. CC and the children land, they go straight to Samarth's house. In Indian tradition, Samarth welcomes them. His white dhoti and mustard kurta were embellished with Indian embroidery. His siblings resided with him. Dr. CC told Samarth his problem and requested he joins them because they needed him.

Dr. CC promised to invent a machine tail for him, the same as Shree Hanuman. Samarth accepted the proposal given by Dr. CC. Ivory, Zara and Samarth were now friends.

They went back to Cosmos X laboratory and started practicing with each other. Dr. CC also invented the machine tail, which functions the same as Shree Hanuman's. Dr. CC also created a cloth for Ivorythrough which she could fly in the air. The cloth is red and has a blue mandala work at the edges. They have created a spot on the terrace of the laboratory where they practice. While practicing, the children thought there should be a name for our team. They searched for a name but couldn't find a perfect one. Then Dr. CC suggested the title "The Quantum Trio." He explained that Quantum means a minimal quantity of electromagnetic energy, and aTrio implies a group of three people.

CHAPTER NINE

The Journey to Kepler-452b

Dr. CC was now waiting to speak to his brother and tell him that he has created a team of 3 of age 14 - 15 years. The team's name is 'The Quantum Trio.' When he said Albus everything, he asked, "but why only three?" Albus replied, "Because the machine I created to transport people from Earth to another planet can only carry five persons at once." Albus continues, "And I want you to complete my project. When I was kidnapped, I broke the TransportXY. It's the name of it. It is kept on the terrace. You must repair the motherboard and connect it to a device from which only pure oxygen passes. Please create the device and speak to me again." The call declines with a beep. Dr. CC went to his home's terrace, then repaired themotherboard and inscribed "TransportXY."

Dr. CC searched the books and found that Hydrogen and Oxygen can be produced through a method known as electrolysis. In the process, Hydrogen and Oxygen can be created by passing an electric current through water and collecting the two gases as they bubble off. Hydrogen forms at the negative terminal, and oxygen at the positive terminal. It produces very pure Hydrogen and Oxygen. Dr. CC passes oxygen through TransportXY, and TransportXY starts! Dr. CC spoke to Albus and informed him that he had repaired it and now wants to know how to function it. Albus replied that you must write 5683999A on the top and come to the centre of the TransportXY. You will be teleported to Arth2010. Albus said one important thing, "The Code for Earth is 05998Z. You will not have to carry oxygen cylinders" Albus does the coding and programmingwork. TransportXY is a hollow cuboid. When it is started, blue light passes through it, and you have to write a specified code on the top. And you will be teleported to any other planet. Dr. CC first tried to go alone to Kepler-452b, but accidentally, he wrote another code, and now he was on Mars. When Dr. CC was about to die, he went back to Earth. Its date is December 30, 2022, at precisely 11:59 PM, when Dr. CC with The Quantum Trio headed off to

Kepler-452b, approximately two light-years from Earth. They teleported on Kepler-452b on 31ˢᵗ December 2022. They teleported into the ground. It was the same as Earth, but when they looked up at the sky. They realized that the sky was virtual. They looked around and realized that everything around them was virtual and generated by any device. Then an alarm rang, and they got panic and went back to Earth in trepidation. Dr. CC called Albus and told him everything about the alarm, then asked what they should do so that no one would recognize them and where they should meet Albus. Albus replied that the alarm was used to tell the people that it was morning and wake up. Albus continues, "You just have to come on a tree on which yellow and red gradient apples are growing and say 'Konishiva.' Ok!" call declined!

CHAPTER TEN

THE QUANTUM TRIO MET SUPER MINDS

Now It's exactly 11:59 PM on 31ˢᵗ December 2022. They again went to Kepler-452b on the same ground and walked nearby; they saw a real tree on which five apples of the yellow and red gradient were present. Dr. CC and The Quantum Trio yelled, "Konishiva." At the next moment, Albus emerges from the tree trunk. Albus was wearing a round shape sci-fi tool in his eyes. He wore a silver chest plate with a black cross in the centre. His chest plate reached to his knees from the right side. His pant is made from titanium, and his helmet is made from tungsten.

Albus hugged Dr. CC. Albus' eyes got wet when he saw all of them. Dr. CC introduced The Quantum Trio to Albus. Albus was so glad to hear about the superpowers of the children. Dr. CC asked, "Why were you kidnapped, and who kidnapped you?"

Albus replied, "The - leader kidnapped me. His name is Draven. He did not kidnap only me but also every alive person with IQ above 160. He is ruthless. Likewise, he wants every super mind to work for him. " Albus continued, "If anyone disagreed to work for him, he used his right arm through which high green radiation passes to kill." Another man comes from the side. He said it was carbon monoxide gas which is poisonous. I am Prof. Thelium. I am from Mars in Andromeda Galaxy."

Samarth asked, -How did you come here?" Prof. Thelium replied I was the first-person Draven kidnapped." Prof. Thelium continued, "I was working on a project related to molecular oxygen gas when a blue light came when I came close to it; I went on this planet." Zara asked, "Do they also speak English?" Albusreplied, "No, they speak another language named the Herosh. We communicate via this device which Prof. Thelium built." Prof. Thelium said, "Its name is Commu. We all speak a different language here, but Commu taught everyone English." Ivory asked, "How does Commu work?"

Commu itself replied in a robotic voice, "When anyone starts me and speaks in their native language or mainly in English, I convert it into the Herosh language and speak it." Commu is a simple black box with an X mark on the sides with bright blue colour. It can fly in the air. Dr. CC asked, "On what thing are you working?" Prof. Thelium replied, "He wanted a gun that could take one life, and if anyone has a superpower, it could take it and fill it in a capsule. It is ready, and it is with Draven. We had to make it to save our lives. Otherwise, we wouldn't make it at any cost." Ivory and Zara asked, "How many soldiers are there in Draven's army?".

CHAPTER ELEVEN

ABOUT THE DARKEST VILLAIN

Albus replied, "The army consists not of people but of robots, big guns, and sci-fi weapons. They work on their own. There are around 100 million soldiers in his army." Prof. Thelium continued, -The robots are the citizen of Gautier-432v. We call arth2010 as Gautier-432v on Mars. Arth2010 was a happy world. But due to development, the feelings got over in them. By the time they became robots. They have no feelings. One day Draven came across arth2010 from any other planet close to black hole. " Prof. Thelium continued, "He stayed here and said the black hole engulfed his world. He had a feeling and a super mind. He built trust in the people with ease and quickly. By that time, He became the leader of this planet. He has three gemstones in his body. One in his chest, second in his right arm and third in his left arm. While these three gemstones are fixed in his body, he is alive. These gemstones should be broken simultaneously, with the same power. Draven is now 500 million years of age." Albus continued," These three stone is the main power of Draven. A black-light comes from two of the side stones. This black light can fly anything up in the sky. The centre gemstone can control anyone's body. It is almost impossible to vanquish him.

CHAPTER TWELVE

PREPARATION

Dr. CC asked, "So what's the plan? We have just three teenagers. How will they fight with his huge and high-tech army? I am so worried about them." Prof. Thelium answered, "Don't worry; we also have a huge army." Albus replied, "Every scientist here has asked anyone from his/her planet to make an army and come to arth2010." Zara yelled, -Someone has come from a hole behind you!!"

Prof. Thelium said, "Congratulations, Dr. Xelium; they have come." Albus said, "My brother, everyone has come. Come along with me!" They all went into a hexagon tent. Many people from different planets gathered together to fight with Draven. Albus sought the attention of everyone present there.

Albus announced, "All of you here have a device in your ears. This device will translate my language into your language called Commu. It's a social problem for everyone. Draven wants to conquer every planet. We don't know the reason, but it's a huge problem. Everyone here is a warrior from now. Your age doesn't matter. God chooses you to fight for your civilization.

We have a plan, but it is not perfect. If anyone is up with an idea, please come in front. Prof. Thelium will continue from now on." Prof. Thelium said, "The army will be divided into four groups. Every group will have one leader. The Groups are marked as X, Y, Z and A.

Team X will attack from the bottom of the main building. Team Y will attack from the back gate. Team Z will be teleported just behind Draven's army chief. Now, team A will blast the terrace and land opposite Draven.

*Prof. Molland from Cygnus A galaxy will continue." Prof. Molland said, "Team X leader is *768*l from the Golimar planet in Milky way galaxy." Prof. Molland continued, "*768*l, please come on the stage.*

Team Y's leader is Tholium, the son of Prof. Thelium. Team Z's leader is Zara from Earth in the Milky way galaxy. Team A's leader is Samarth from Earth in the Milky way galaxy." Teams were divided. Ivory was in Team Z.

Zara announced Ivory as her assistant leader. Albus said, "If anyone wants to give any idea, please come forward." Ivory said, "We should give everyone a weapon." Prof. Molland said, "Great idea, young one!" Everyone got their weapons. Ivory received a titanium axe. Zara received another wand, whereas Samarth received Metalloid's modified metal tail. Metalloid is a metal discovered on Mars in the Andromeda Galaxy.

CHAPTER THIRTEEN

THE GREAT WAR BEGIN

It's the 1st day of the year in Arth2010; today, everyone will fight with Draven, and it's a vast army. The entire team was prepared in their respective positions. Dr. CC. Team Y blew the horn and entered through the back door.

Everyone there got panic and started to fire on Team Y. On the second whistle, Team Z was teleported. Ivory controlled the chief's mind and asked him to join Team Z. Chief ordered the same, and now Draven's army is with Team Z.

No one of our armies was killed. Team Y, along with Team Z, entered the main hall. As soon as they entered the main entrance, they saw the ground chess. Draven was standing in the king's position.

Draven yelled in his language and translated by Commu, " I got the news! That some small and cute kids have come to fight with me." Draven continued, "There are simple rules of chess. You are already placed in your positions, and your king is Dr. Cyrus Celdon, often known as Dr. CC.

Here Dr. CC will order you all to walk and fight." Ivory was in the queen's position. Zara was in the rook position. Dr. CC started the game, and at the starting only, we lost many of our friends. Only Zara, Ivory, two pawns, one bishop, and two knights were left, and Dr. CC was left. Dr. CC made his most robust strategy and checkmated Draven. Draven was almost on the deathbed. Draven shouted, "See you next time!" and got disappeared. All the doors were closed, and they got trapped in that room. Zara called, 'Team X! Near the gate'.

*At the next moment, *768*l, along with his army, broke the gate. They all went to the court of Draven. It was designed as the Roman Empire. When one person from Team X went to a pole, she got hit by a wall. A bullet hurt Dr. CC, and Zara healed Dr. CC with CX. Ivory said that it was a trap.*

We have to destroy these walls to reach Draven. Then another beam hit another warrior of Team Z. He died instantly, and a beam carried a message. That message said, "Power of Electricity." No one had any idea about that message. A person from the side took out his beam gun and fired toward the wall. Wall blasted, and now they were in front of Draven. Draven took out a gun and fired at the teams.

Through the gun's beam, every person touched by it breathed their last breath. Draven got their powers as soon as they died. Dr. CC chanted the name of the Ram. At the second moment, Samarth was in front of Dr. CC. Samarth used his tail and grabbed Draven like candy. Samarth was taking the gun; Draven gave an electric shock to Samarthand disappeared.

Now almost 3/4ᵗʰ army was dead. Everyone was depressed. Albus, along with all scientists, asked for an apology from everyone. Prof. Molland said, "It was all the plan of Draven. Draven only ordered us to invite you all to arth2010 so that he could get the superpower of you all." Prof. Thelium continued, "He only told us to invite teenagers because it is easy to kill teenagers. He threatened us about our lives. We are so sorry about you all. Now will not be in his plan. Now we will overpower him and return to our planets happily. Even though Draven is also not that bad." Mr. Tholium asked, "Why, dad?"

CHAPTER FOURTEEN

THE BACKSTORY

It was the time when five years old Draven was threatened by his civilization. The gravitational pull of the enormous black hole continuously pulled his planet. The leader of his world ran away from this problem.

In a few days, a new leader was chosen. He said they should leave this planet behind and settle in a new one. But there was one problem they had only a few spacecrafts. The new leader ordered that we would kill people of smaller castes and other people would travel in the spacecraft. Smaller castes denied it, but the leader killed everyone.

In this massacre, Draven's family was also killed. On his planet, smaller castes had only one gemstone in their chest, whereas higher castes were born with three jewels. Draven had only one. When smaller castes were, one was killed and disappeared himself. Sadly, his parents were killed.

Draven ran towards his parents. As soon as he touched his parents' gemstone, the gemstone became attached to his arms, and he became like he is now. Due to the three jewels, he could enter the spacecraft. In the spaceship, the leader was also sitting. The spaceship took a lot of time to reach any destination.

By that time, Draven had grown older. One day in the space probe, he decided to fight with all the upper classes. He did so, but when he tried to kill the leader, he got teleported into another space capsule. From there, Draven took the flying saucers controls and came to arth2010. Draven only kept the name of this planet.

Draven's main motive is to make the world's most enormous army, conquer every world, and show it to the leader. Draven has conquered the world of that planet, but he now wants to destroy every person who discriminates by the caste system. His goal is superb, but his way of achieving it is the worst.

CHAPTER FIFTEEN

THE FINAL WARNING

Zara said, "Let's go and make Draven understand his way and let him be the one to make the decision. We should not attack without any warning. Only we will attack him if he disagrees with our offer. It is his last chance." Another child asked, "Where is he?" Prof. Molland answered, "He is in the next room." Dr. Xelium said that his next plan is that when we enter the next room, Prof. Albus will press the button in his helmet and make a cage of ultraviolet rays. By which no one could run here and there, and he could kill each one of us without any headache.

Albus took out his helmet and ordered everyone to destroy it. Everyone used their powers and destroyed the helmet. At last, a rare metal of arth2010 was found. Dr. CC took that rare metal and kept it in his briefcase. Everyone set foot in the next room. It was not any room; It was an open field. Draven said, "Ok, you all are here." Ivory took the opportunity and said, "It's your final warning, Draven! Your motive is excellent, but you are making harm other people too. We will help you achieve your goal if you leave our professors.

We all totally agree with your motive. Please agree with us; otherwise, we have to take a wrong step against you, and we don't want to kill a person with great motive." Draven said, "You all are such good people; I have done wrong with you all; I am in your guidance from now." Draven turned around and then said with an evil laugh, "You all thought I would change myself, but no, I have no problem being evil. I was a good person many centuries ago, but now I am an evil personality and am happy with it. Fire! Fire! Fire! Fire! Fire!"

CHAPTER SIXTEEN

THE END OF THE BATTLE

At the very next moment, a cannonball hits Prof. Molland, and he has breathed his last breath. Dr. CC said, "Make a rhombus. Electric power at the first row and fire one at the second. Make two trident shapes with all the armies." Samarth took Dr. CC, as well as other professors, on the top of a wall.

Everyone was ready in their positions. At the next moment, a group of robots ran toward the army. The chief was in a flying saucer. Ivory flew toward the head and killed the leader with her axe.

Ivory took the flying saucer in her control and brought many people on it. Zara ordered to run towards the robot. Zara was running behind everyone to heal the injured one. This strategy was getting overloaded on Draven. Draven came towards Ivory and controlled her body. Draven ordered Ivory to control Tholium mind and tell him to kill his father. Ivory did it, and Tholium killed his father.

Prof. Thelium fell, and now Draven has chosen the same trick to kill everyone. Samarth took a long jump toward the flying saucer. Samarth took Ivory's axe and placed it in between the ray. The ray scatters, and Draven stops himself. At the next moment, Draven disappears and is now at the edge of the field. Now our army is led by killing every robot present there. But now our military had only 20 people left, including The Quantum Trio, Tholium and many more.

Draven took out his gun and killed everyone. Draven was just about to take all the power in his body. Then Tholium asked The Quantum Trio to hold Draven so that he could take the gun and destroy it. Samarth took his tail and held Draven's waist; Ivory sat on his head, and Zara used her wand to make a ring around his arms and legs. Tholium took the gun and gave it to Dr. CC, and Dr. CC made a short circuit in the weapon. Albus told Dr. CC, "By destroying the gun, Draven would lose all the power gained by this weapon in a few minutes."

But Tholium was killed by a mixture of fire, electricity, air, land and many more used by Draven. Now only The Quantum Trio was left, and now Draven became free.

Now Draven doesn't have any other power than anyone else. Ivory ran towards Draven and used her axe to do damage to Draven. Draven kicked her, but behind her, all the professors and scientists were present. Ivory took her axe and made a massive attack on the centre gemstone of Draven. Samarth and Zara also accompanied her.

The Quantum Trio took a back step and made a significant attack on three of the gemstones. Draven was now weak against all of them. Draven was now almost on the deathbed.

Draven said, "I am now at my end, but I want you all to convey my message to all the people on your planet not to discriminate anyone on any basis.". Draven continues, I had chosen the wrong path, so I received a deadly and horrible death.

You all gave me another chance, but I was not ready. I have two powers from my parent to kill anyone by thinking his name with death and reborning one person by saying Rebornish and his name.

I have completed my task by killing the leader and making alive Tholium." Draven gave up, and now Draven was dead. The virtual sky was gone. The robots who were killed were now alive, and now they had feelings. Dr. CC, Albus and other scientists made a leader for Arth2010. They also built a structure of Draven for having correct thinking about discrimination. They also created a statue of The Quantum Trio and Tholium. Furthermore, they also constructed a wall on which the names of those killed during the war were written. The society of Arth2010 also gave everyone a lot of technology, so they could become high-tech.

CHAPTER SEVENTEEN

RETURN TO THE HOME

It was time to go back home. Everyone hugged each other for the last time. Tholium told Albus he would not return to his planet because he killed his father. Albus told Tholium that he should go to his world and live with his family. Tholium told Albus that he had no one on his planet. He wanted to go with Albus. He agreed to Tholium.

The Quantum Trio - Helping Their World

They all went to Earth, but now Tholium showed his natural face. He took all the high-tech things and tried to conquer Earth. The Quantum Trio will now save their world.

About The Author

Atharv Garg

Atharv Garg at the very early age of 12, successfully launched his debut novel, 'The Quantum Trio - Fight for The Super minds.' He is a passionate writer with a super scientific mind.

Email – gargsonu981@gmail.com and gargatharv2010@gmail.com
Phone - 9953944012 and 9312208125
Instagram - atharv.garg10